P9-AFK-692

DIGGER and TOM!

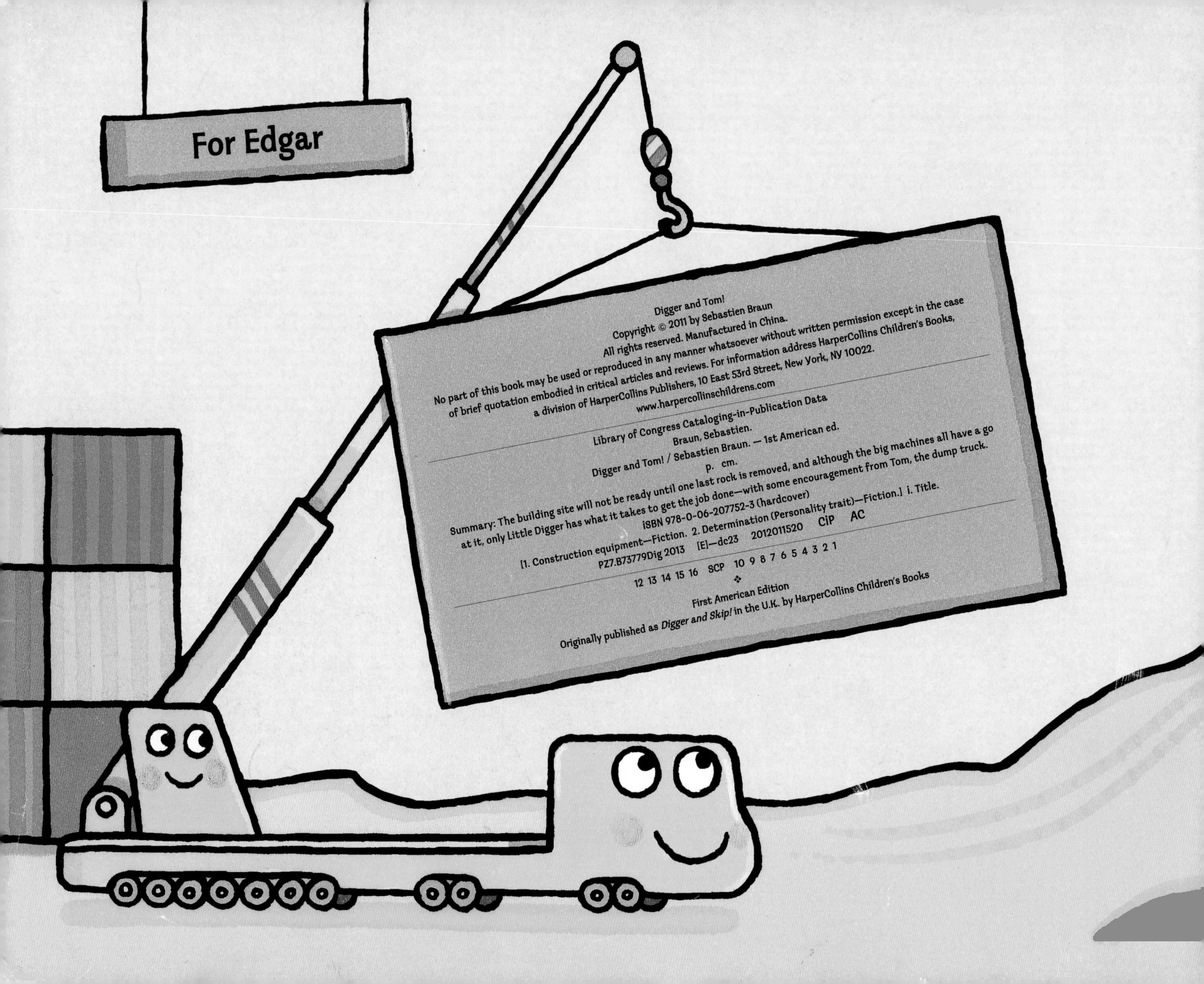

For Edgar

Digger and Tom!

For information address HarperCollins Children's Books, a division of HarperCollins Publishers, 10 East 53rd Street, New York, NY 10022.
www.harpercollinschildrens.com

Library of Congress Cataloging-in-Publication Data
Braun, Sebastien.
Digger and Tom! / Sebastien Braun. — 1st American ed.
p. cm.
Summary: The building site will not be ready until one last rock is removed, and although the big machines all have a go at it, only Little Digger has what it takes to get the job done—with some encouragement from Tom, the dump truck.
ISBN 978-0-06-207752-3 (hardcover)
[1. Construction equipment—Fiction. 2. Determination (Personality trait)—Fiction.] I. Title.
PZ7.B73779Dig 2013 [E]—dc23 2012011520 CIP AC

12 13 14 15 16 SCP 10 9 8 7 6 5 4 3 2 1
❖
First American Edition

Originally published as *Digger and Skip!* in the U.K. by HarperCollins Children's Books

DIGGER and TOM!

by Sebastien Braun

HARPER
An Imprint of HarperCollins*Publishers*

Dig!

Dig!

Dig!

This is Digger. Hello, Digger!

He is a very busy little digging machine.

Every day Digger tries his best to
help out at the construction site . . .

Digger started digging.
Dig!
Dig! Dig!
But the rock stayed
stuck in the mud.

"It's much

bigger

than I thought," puffed Digger.

"Keep trying," said Tom.

"You can do it!"

Just then, the other
machines gathered around.
"Leave the hard work to the experts now,
Digger," Chuck, the bulldozer, said bossily.

First Basher, the demolition vehicle, tried smashing the rock.

Then Roland, the steamroller, tried flattening it.

"Heave!" said Chuck,
pushing with all his might.
Heave!
Heave!
Finally, Grabber, the
truck crane, had a turn.
Clank!
Clank!
Clank!
But it was no use.
The rock wouldn't budge.

"Let's take a break before we try again," said Chuck. "The construction site's not safe if we leave the rock like this."

Tom looked at Digger. . . .

"Why don't you
have another try?"
Tom whispered kindly.
"You're a digger. Digging's
what you do best!"

And so, while the others rested, Digger got to work.

Dig!

He dug deeper . . .
and deeper . . .

Dig!

and deeper . . .

until, at last, the rock was free!

"You did it!"

cried Tom.

The other machines were amazed.

"Well done, Digger!"

they cheered.

At last, they could finish cleaning the site . . . together.

Clank!

Clank! Clank!

Brrrm! Brrrm!

Whirr!
Whirr!

It had been a long, hard day.

"What a team!"

said Tom.

"What fun!"

said Digger.

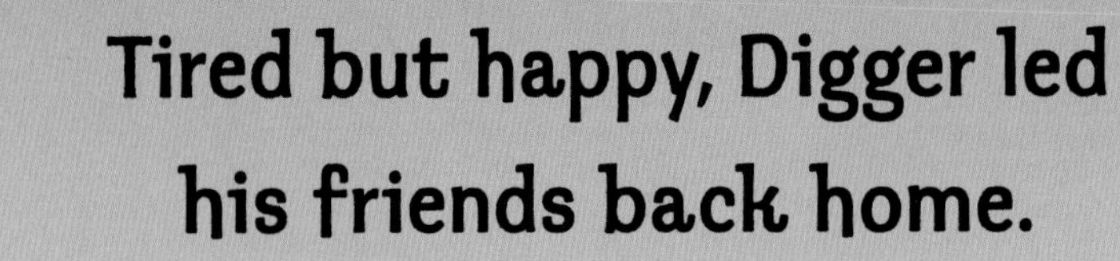

Tired but happy, Digger led
his friends back home.

"Thank you for believing in me, Tom," said Digger as they settled down for the night.

"Everyone on our team is special," said Tom, "but we couldn't have done the job without you!"

Digger smiled sleepily. . . .

"It's all in a day's work," he said.